# The Berenstain Bears®

## Friendship Blessings

## Collection

**by Jan and Mike Berenstain**

ZONDER**kidz**

*Living Lights™*
*A Faith Story*

ZONDERKIDZ

*The Berenstain Bears® Friendship Blessings Collection*

Copyright © 2016 by Berenstain Publishing, Inc.
Illustrations © 2016 by Berenstain Publishing, Inc.

Requests for information should be addressed to:
Zonderkidz, 3900 *Sparks Dr. SE, Grand Rapids, Michigan* 49546

ISBN 978-0-310-75338-4 (hardcover)

The Berenstain Bears® Perfect Fishing Spot ISBN 978-0-310-72276-2 (2011)
The Berenstain Bears® Reap the Harvest ISBN 978-0-310-72277-9 (2011)
The Berenstain Bears® Faithful Friends ISBN 978-0-310-71253-4 (2009)
The Berenstain Bears® Kindness Counts ISBN 978-0-310-71257-2 (2010)
The Berenstain Bears® God Made You Special ISBN 978-0-310-73483-3 (2014)

*Editor: Mary Hassinger*
*Design: Cindy Davis*

*Printed in China*

16  17  18  19  20  21 /LPC/ 21  20  19  18  17  16  15  14  13  12  11  10  9  8  7  6  5  4  3  2  1

# The Berenstain Bears'
# PERFECT FISHING SPOT

*She speaks with wisdom,*
*and faithful instruction is on her tongue.*
*She watches over the affairs of her household ...*

—Proverbs 31:26–27

by Stan and Jan Berenstain
with Mike Berenstain

ZONDERkidz

Living Lights
A Faith Story

Beginning Reader

Do you know what I wish?
I wish that for dinner
we could have fish.

A fine, fat fish, tender and sweet.
There is nothing better
in the world to eat!
Thanks be to God
for that delicious treat!

A fish would be fine.
But there's no need to fuss.
Just go and buy one
from Grizzly Gus.

GRIZZLY GUS
FISH

May Sister and I come with you, Dad?

Yes, indeed.
Of course, my lad.
Spending time with you two
makes my heart glad!

But, Papa!
Ma said go to Grizzly Gus!

That's true, my son.
But just between us,
if you want a fish
that's tender and sweet,
a fish that's a wonderful treat
for a bear to eat—

GRIZZLY
FISH

then dig up some
worms, get out your pole,

and head for your favorite
fishing hole.

9

Your fishing hole
looks small, Papa Bear.
Can there really be
a big fish in there?

Of course there can.
I've got one now!
Just watch your dad.
He'll show you how
to catch a fish
that's tender and sweet,
a fish that's a treat
for a bear to eat!

Papa, that fish
may be tender and sweet,
but it's much too small
for us to eat.

Hmm. The big ones have all
been caught, you see,
caught years ago
by guess who? ME!

I know a better
fishing spot!

I can taste that fish,
tender, hot,
a fish to do
our family proud...

14

But Pa, it says
NO FISHING ALLOWED!

NO FISHING

But who will know
if I drop my hook?

*He* will, Pa!
The fish warden! Look!

FISH
WARDEN

I see, I see.
Good day to you!
Er...my cubs and I
were enjoying the view!
So sorry! God bless!
Such a good job you do!

17

This fish, Dad,
will you catch it soon?
I think it must be
after noon!

Don't bother me
with questions, please.
I know a spot
just past those trees!

18

Look, cubs! Look!
I've got a bite!
Whatever I've hooked,
just look at it fight!

Look how it thrashes!
Look how it sloshes!

20

Dad, that isn't a fish!
It's a pair of galoshes!

21

This way, cubs!
Follow me!
We will get our fish
from the deep blue sea!
God provides, he'll make sure
we have what we need!

BOATS
RENTED

22

Look at them all!
They'll sink our boat!
Throw 'em back!
We must stay afloat!

Boat and all!
In a great big net!
We're in the air
and very wet!

We're coming down
on a great big boat—
the biggest
fishing boat afloat!

You got caught with our fish.
Sorry about that!
Excuse me, sir—
but that's one of ours
under your hat!

Pa, we still have
a fish to get!
We have not caught
our dinner yet!

No problem, son.
No need to fuss!
We'll buy our fish
from Grizzly Gus!

BUY OUR FISH
FROM GRIZZLY GUS?

31

My best advice
to both of you
is to do what Mama
says to do!

God's blessed Gus with
the perfect fishing spot.
We never really
had a shot.

33

Ah! A fish that's tender.
A fish that's sweet.
A fish that's good
for a bear family to eat!
God bless this food.
God bless this treat!

*... Imitate those who through faith and patience inherit what has been promised.*

—Hebrews 6:12

# The Berenstain Bears®

# REAP THE HARVEST

by Stan and Jan Berenstain
with Mike Berenstain

 ZONDERkidz  Beginning Reader

It was summertime. School was closed for the year. Brother and Sister Bear were walking down a dusty road. They were thinking about how they should spend their summer vacation.

"We could just play," said Sister.

"Playing is fine," said Brother. "But playing all the time would be boring."

"We could go swimming," said Sister.

"Swimming is fine," said Brother.
"But we can't go swimming every day."

"We could go to the library," said Sister.

"Yes," said Brother. "Mama takes us to the library every Saturday. But what will we do the rest of the week?"

"Maybe we could get a job!" said Sister. "Papa says according to Proverbs, 'All hard work brings a profit.' Maybe we can make some money."

"That's a good idea," said Brother. "But what kind of job could we get? We're just cubs."

That's when they saw the sign. It was
hanging on Farmer Ben's front gate. It said:
HELP WANTED. SEE FARMER BEN.

"Well, yes," said Farmer Ben. "I do need help. But I was thinking of someone older. What could you cubs do to help?"

45

"All kinds of things," said the cubs.

"We could sweep the barn,

feed the chickens,

collect the eggs

slop the hogs,

HERE BOSSIE

call the cows,

and make sure the bull pen is locked tight."

"Hmmm," said Farmer Ben. He thought for a while. Then he said, "All right. The job is yours. Here are some brooms. You can start by sweeping the barn."

"There's just one thing," said Sister. "If this is a job, we should get paid."

"Yes," said Brother. "How much will you pay us?"

"Hmmm," said Ben. "See that field? That's my cornfield, and corn is my cash crop."

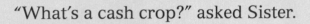

"What's a cash crop?" asked Sister.

"A cash crop is what a farmer grows to make money," said Brother.

51

"I'll tell you what," said Ben. He took a piece of string and some sticks and marked off a corner of the field.

"If you do a good job, I'll pay you the money I get for all the corn that grows in that corner of the field."

"How much will that be?" asked Sister.

"Depends," said Farmer Ben.

"Depends on what?" asked Brother.

"Depends on how much rain the Good Lord sends our way," said Ben. "Not too little; not too much. Depends on cornbugs. In a bad year, cornbugs can ruin a crop. Depends on keeping the crows from eating the seed—

that's why I'm making this scarecrow."

"So we won't know how much money we'll earn until the end of the summer," said Sister.

"No more than I will," said Farmer Ben. "That's the way it is with farming. Same way it is with faith … our true reward comes later on—in God's good time."

So the cubs went to work.

They swept the barn.

They fed
the chickens.

They collected the eggs.

They slopped the hogs.

They called the cows.

HERE BOSSIE

They made sure the bull pen was locked tight.

57

And they kept a close watch on their corner of the cornfield!

Brother watched the sky for rain.

Sister had bad dreams about cornbugs.

And when the crows were no longer afraid of Farmer Ben's scarecrow, Brother and Sister made a scarier one. It even scared Farmer Ben.

Working on the farm was hard, but it was fun too.

Brother and Sister both loved and respected all of God's creatures. And they made friends with the animals—

the chickens,

the pigs,

the cows.

Even Ben's big bull seemed
to like Brother and Sister.

But the best thing was having their own corner of the cornfield. The corn grew straight and tall and healthy.

"Farmer Ben told me the book of Timothy says, 'The hardworking farmer should be the first to receive a share of the crops,'" quoted Brother.

"Yessir," said Ben as he got ready to harvest the corn. "This is the finest cash crop I've grown in years. You cubs are going to do all right."

And they did. Their corner of the cornfield earned them many, many dollars. The farm had been blessed with a fine harvest indeed.

"Well," said Farmer Ben as he paid the cubs, "you should be proud of the good job you did all summer. Now don't spend it all in one place."

"We won't," said Brother. "But we will *put* it all in one place—the bank!"

"That's right," said Sister. "It took us a long time to earn this money. We want to keep it at least as long as it took to earn it."

"Do not forsake your friend."

—Proverbs 27:10

# The Berenstain Bears.
# Faithful Friends

written by Jan and Mike Berenstain

Living Lights™
A Faith Story

ZONDERkidz

Lizzy Bruin was Sister Bear's very best friend. It seemed like they had been best friends for a very long time.

Lizzy Bruin and Sister Bear had been through a lot together. Once they had a slumber party that got a little out of hand.

They were in the school play that time Brother forgot his lines.

They played dress up
and dolls, and rode their
bikes, and picked flowers,
and rolled down hills, and
giggled.

Sister was glad she had such a good friend. She could always rely on Lizzy to be there for her. They hardly ever fought or argued. Not, that is, until Sister started to spend more time with Suzy MacGrizzie.

Suzy was a new cub in town. At first, Sister and her friends didn't pay much attention to Suzy. But then, Sister noticed how lonely Suzy was and invited her to play. From then on, Suzy was part of Sister's little group.

All of Sister's friends, including Lizzy, liked Suzy. She was one more cub to spend time with and enjoy.

But Suzy was a little different from the other cubs. For one thing, she read an awful lot. And she was interested in different things—science, for instance. Suzy invited Sister over one night to look at the sky. Suzy pointed her telescope up at the moon.

"Wow!" said Sister, looking into the eyepiece. "It looks so close." She could actually see mountains and valleys and craters on the moon. It was very interesting.

One day, Suzy asked Sister to go on a butterfly hunt with her. They took butterfly nets and went out into the fields.

Sister caught a big yellow butterfly with black stripes. Suzy caught one that had bright red and blue spots on it and long swallowtails. It was very beautiful. After they studied the butterflies for a while, they let them go, and the butterflies sailed up into the sky over the trees.

"They're so pretty!" said Sister.

On their way back, Suzy and Sister ran into Lizzy and their friends Anna and Millie. They were all carrying their Bearbie dolls. "Hiya, gang!" called Sister when she saw them. "Suzy and I were out catching butterflies. You should have seen the big yellow one I got!"

"Yeah, great," said Lizzy. "Well, see you, I guess."
"Wait a minute," said Sister. "Where are you all going?"
"We're going over to my garage to play Bearbie dolls," said Lizzy.
"Can Suzy and I come too?" asked Sister.

"It looks like you two are already pretty busy," said Lizzy. "Come on, girls." With that, Lizzy and her friends went on their way.

"How do you like that?" said Sister, hurt and angry. "Who does she think she is? Come on, Suzy, we'll play over at my house. Who needs them, anyway?"

When they got to the Bear family's tree house, Suzy and Sister found Brother Bear and Cousin Fred getting out their fishing tackle.

"Lizzy and your friends were here looking for you," Brother said. "I told them you were playing with Suzy. Lizzy didn't seem very happy."

"That Lizzy Bruin!" said Sister, annoyed. "What business is it of hers who I play with?"

"I guess she's jealous," said Brother.

"Jealous?" said Sister, puzzled.

"Sure," said Brother. "She's been your best friend for years. You mean a lot to her. She's just worried that maybe you don't like her as much as you used to."

"Oh," said Sister, "that's silly!" It was true that she liked her new friend, Suzy. But Lizzy would always be her best friend.

"What should I do?" Sister wondered.

Cousin Fred spoke up. "You know what the Bible says: 'Wounds from a friend can be trusted.'" Fred liked to memorize things.

"Huh?" said both Sister and Brother. "What does that mean?"

Suzy answered—she liked to memorize things too. "I think it means that when a friend who loves you hurts your feelings, you need to find out what is bothering her."

"Yes," Fred nodded. "And the Bible also says that we shouldn't stay angry with our friends. God wants us to make up with them if we have an argument."

"Oh," said Sister, thoughtfully.

"I have an idea," said Brother. "Fred and I were about to go fishing. Why don't we grab some extra fishing gear and go over to Lizzy's? We can see if they would all like to go fishing with us."

"Great!" said Sister. Suzy grinned.

So they all stopped by Lizzy's garage on their way to the fishing hole.

"Hey, Lizzy!" called Sister. "Do you and Anna and Millie want to go fishing with us?"

Lizzy acted like she wasn't so sure. But Anna and Millie were all for it, and Lizzy certainly didn't want to be left out.

Soon, they were all down at the fishing hole. Lizzy cast her line out into the middle of the pond and got her line into a terrible tangle.

"Here, let me help you, Lizzy," said Sister, taking her fishing rod. "I'll untangle it for you."

"Wow, thanks!" said Lizzy. "You're a real friend, Sister."

"I always have been and I always will be!" said Sister, giving Lizzy a hug.

And together they picked away at the tangled fishing line.

# Activities and Questions from Brother and Sister Bear

Talk about it:

1. How can you invite new friends into your friend group?

2. Have you ever felt left out by a friend? What do you think God would want you to do when that happens?

3. Do you like to do different things with different friends? Name some things you do differently.

Get out and do it:

1. Design a constellation—a group of stars that make a picture. Tape a piece of black paper over the end of an empty toilet paper tube. Use a pin to poke holes in the paper in a design. Look through the tube at a light to see your constellation design.

2. Draw a fish outline. Fill the outline with crayon textures, cut paper, and other materials to create eyes, mouth, and textured scales and fins.

3. Play Follow the Leader. Take turns being the leader.

# The Berenstain Bears®
# Kindness Counts

written by Jan and Mike Berenstain

ZONDER**kidz**

Living Lights™
A Faith Story

Brother Bear was a bear of many interests. He enjoyed sports such as baseball, soccer, football, and basketball. He liked to draw and paint, and he was interested in science. He had hobbies like collecting stamps and baseball cards, and he enjoyed fishing and playing video games. But the thing he enjoyed most of all was building model airplanes.

He started building models with Papa when he was very young. At first, they made simple plastic models. But, soon, they were creating flying models out of lightweight wood and paper. Before long, Brother could build models all by himself.

He kept building bigger and better models that could fly longer, farther, and higher. On trips to the park with Sister Bear, he always took along his latest model for flight trials. It was a thrill to wind its propeller for the first time, let it go, and watch it fly across the park.

One Saturday afternoon, Brother tried out his latest creation, a big model plane painted bright red called *The Meteor*. He set it down on the grass and wound the propeller. Sister joined some of her friends nearby. One of them was minding her younger brother, Billy. He was playing with a small model plane like the ones Brother had when he was little.

When Billy saw Brother's big new plane, he came over to take a look.

"Wow!" he said. "That's beautiful!"

"Thanks! She's called *The Meteor*. I built her myself," Brother said proudly.

"Wow!" said Billy. "I wish I could build a plane like that."

Brother finished winding the propeller and picked up *The Meteor.*
"Can I help you fly it?" asked Billy.

Brother was proud of his models and careful with them too. They took a long time to build and were easy to break. If you didn't launch them just right, they could take a nosedive and crash.

"Well," said Brother doubtfully, "I don't know…," But he remembered how Papa always let him help out when they were building and flying model planes. That's how he learned—by helping Papa.

"Well," said Brother, "okay. You can help me hold it."

"Oh, boy! Thanks!" said Billy.

Brother knelt down and let Billy hold the model with him.

"Now, remember," said Brother, "don't throw it—let it fly out of your hands. Here we go— one, two, three ... *fly*!"

They both let go, and the big red *Meteor* lifted up and away, its propeller whirring.

"YIPEEE!" yelled Billy. "Look at it fly!"

But Brother was worried. *The Meteor* was climbing up too steeply. As they watched, *The Meteor* rose high above the park. It seemed to pause in midair. Its nose suddenly dipped down, and it went into a dive. *The Meteor* hit the ground with a nasty *crunch*!

113

Brother and Billy ran to the wrecked model. Brother sadly picked it up and looked at the damage. Billy's big sister and the others noticed the excitement and came over.

"Oh, no!" said Billy. "Is it my fault? Did I do something wrong? Did I throw it instead of letting it fly like you said?"

Brother shook his head. "Of course not!" he said. "You did fine. This is my fault. I didn't get the balance right. It's tail heavy. That's why it went up too steep, paused, and dove down. That's called 'stalling.'"

"Are you going to fix it?" asked Billy.

"Sure!" laughed Brother. "'Build 'em, fly 'em, crash 'em, fix 'em!' That's my motto."

"Could I help you?" wondered Billy.

"Now, Billy," said his big sister, "you're too young to help."

But Brother remembered how Papa always used to let him help. That was how he learned about model airplanes.

"That's okay," Brother told Billy's big sister. "I don't mind. I could use a little help."

So Billy came along to the Bears' tree house. Mama and Papa were pleased that Brother was being so kind to young Billy.

"It's just as the Good Book says," Mama said, "'Blessed are the merciful, for they will be shown mercy.'"

"Yes," agreed Papa, "and it also says in the Bible that a kind person benefits himself."

"What does that mean?" wondered Brother.

"It means that no act of kindness is wasted," said Papa. "Any kindness you do will always come back to you."

Blessed are the merciful, for they will be shown mercy.
Matthew 5:7

Every afternoon that week, Billy helped Brother work on the plane. He didn't know very much, but he learned a lot and he had lots of fun. Brother had fun too. He enjoyed teaching, and he liked having a helper who looked up to him.

The next Saturday, *The Meteor* was ready for another flight. Brother and Billy took it down to the park. Everyone came along to watch. They wound *The Meteor's* propeller, held it up, and let it fly. It lifted away and rose in a long, even curve.

"This looks like a good flight!" said Brother.

*The Meteor* flew on and on across the field. Slowly, it came down, landing clear on the other side of the park in a three-point landing. Brother and Billy ran over. It was in perfect shape.

"Hurray!" yelled Billy, jumping up and down.

Brother began to wind up the propeller for another try, but he noticed a group of older cubs coming into the park. They carried a lot of interesting equipment and wore jackets that said "Bear Country Rocket Club." Brother went over to watch. They were setting up a model rocket. They were going to fire it off and let it come down by parachute. Brother was excited.

"Excuse me," he said to the cub in charge, "do you think I could help you launch the rocket?"

The cub shook his head. "Sorry!" he said. "You're too young. It's too dangerous."

Brother walked away sadly. But he noticed that Billy was staying behind. He was talking to the older cub in charge. The older cub called Brother back.

"My cousin, Billy, tells me you let him help with your model plane," said the older cub. Brother just nodded. The older cub smiled. "That was cool. You seem to know a lot about flying and models. I guess you can help out."

So the rocket club
let Brother hold things
for them, carry things for
them, and squirt a little
glue here and there. He
learned a lot and he was
happy. When it was time
to fire off the rocket, they
even let Brother push
the button.

"10, 9, 8, 7, 6, 5, 4, 3, 2, 1 … *fire!*" said the cub in charge, and Brother pushed the button.

There was a loud *WHOOOSH*!

The rocket shot up, leaving a trail of smoke.

High above the park a yellow
parachute popped open, and the
rocket drifted back to earth.

They ran over to it. It was all twisted and scorched.

"Are you going to fix it?" asked Brother.

"Sure," laughed the older cub. "'Build 'em, fly 'em, crash 'em, fix 'em!' That's our motto."

"Could I help you?" asked Brother.

The older cub thought it over. "Sure," he said, slapping Brother on the back. "Why not?"

So, because Brother Bear had shown a little kindness to someone younger than himself, he became the youngest member, ever, of the Bear Country Rocket Club.

And was he ever proud!

# Activities and Questions from Brother and Sister Bear

Talk about it:

1.  Do you have a special talent or hobby? How did you first become interested in this hobby? How did Brother become interested in model airplanes?

2.  Why did Brother hesitate before actually sharing his model airplane with Billy? Why is it sometimes difficult to share something you really like and other times very easy?

3.  Describe a time that you have shown kindness to someone and been shown a kindness in return. Do you think that you need to be rewarded every time you do something nice? Why or why not?

Get out and do it:

1.  Create a poster for your family to hang in a prominent place in the house. Have the following scripture phrase on it: "In everything, do to others what you would want them to do to you." (Matthew 7:12)

2.  Organize a family hobby day. Have each family member share what they enjoy doing the most with the rest of the family. Remember to be kind as you explain directions and show others your hobby.

Jesus said, "Let the little children come to me, and do not hinder them, for the kingdom of heaven belongs to such as these."

—Matthew 19:14

# The Berenstain Bears
## GOD MADE YOU
## SPECIAL

By Mike Berenstain
Based on the characters created by
Stan & Jan Berenstain

ZONDERkidz

Brother and Sister Bear knew God loved them. They knew it because Mama and Papa told them so.

They knew it because Preacher Brown preached about it at church. They knew it, too, because the Bible told them so.

The cubs knew God's love in other ways too. They could feel his love in the world around them. They could feel it in the warm morning sunshine. They could feel it in the cool evening breeze.

They could feel it in the flutter of a butterfly's wing and the quiver of a baby bunny's heartbeat.

But what about all the other cubs in the whole wide world—did God love all of them too?

It just so happened that a couple of those other cubs were about to arrive at the Bear family's tree house. They were Sister's best friend, Lizzy Bruin, and her older brother, Barry. The two families were having a big backyard cookout.

"Here they come!" said Sister, spotting the Bruins' car.

"Terrific!" said Brother.

"'iffic!" said Honey.

But when the Bruins got out of their car, Brother, Sister, and Honey were surprised to see another cub with them. He was about Brother's age. He had a fuzzy head and a happy smile. They wondered who he was.

"This is our nephew, Tommy," said Mrs. Bruin, greeting the Bear family. "He's visiting us for a week."

"Hello, there, Tommy," said Mama Bear. "Welcome to our house."

Tommy seemed shy. He just looked at Mama and smiled.

"Say, 'Hello,' to Mama Bear, Tommy," said Mrs. Bruin.

Tommy was silent for a moment and then said, "Hi!" with a big but bashful grin.

"That's fine, Tommy," said Mrs. Bruin. "Now go and play with the other cubs."

Lizzy took Tommy by the hand and lead him to the backyard where a game of baseball was getting started.

Mrs. Bruin took Mama to one side.

"I should explain about Tommy," she said. "He may seem a little young for his age. He's very happy and friendly and he's the same age as Brother and Barry. But he acts younger—more like little Honey Bear."

"I understand," said Mama. "He seems like a very sweet cub. We're very glad to meet him and have him here for our cookout."

Behind the tree house, the cubs started their game. Brother, Lizzy, and Honey were on one team and Barry, Sister, and Tommy were on the other. Brother's team was up first. Barry was pitching, Sister catching, and Tommy was out in the field. Right away, Lizzy whacked a ball out toward Tommy.

"Grab it, Tommy!" called Barry.

But Tommy didn't grab the baseball. He watched it roll by.

"Go get it, Tommy!" encouraged Barry.

Tommy ran after the ball and picked it up. Lizzy ran around the bases heading for second. Tommy chased after her.

"Go, Tommy boy, go!" yelled Barry.

Lizzy rounded second but Tommy caught up with her. He tagged her with the ball.

"Yer out!" said Barry.
Sister was puzzled.

"Hey, Barry," she said. "Why did Tommy let the ball go past and then run with it instead of throwing to second? That's what he should have done."

"Tommy has his own way of doing things," said Barry. "He's just a little different, that's all. Let's play ball."

The cubs went on with their game. But they soon lost two of their players. Tommy noticed a butterfly flitting across the field. He started to chase it. Honey thought this looked like more fun than baseball too and joined him.

"We just lost our outfielders," said Brother.

"Never mind," said Lizzy. "We can play without them."

Brother and Sister shrugged. If it was okay with Lizzy and Barry, it was okay with them. The game went on.

Soon, Papa Bear called, "The food's almost ready! Come and help out."
The cubs could smell the hamburgers and hotdogs cooking.
"Okay!" they called.

While Sister was helping set the picnic table she grew thoughtful.

"Mama," she said, "Tommy seems sort of different. He doesn't act like our other cub friends. Why is he like that?"

"Well, Sister," said Mama. "We are all a little different from each other. We don't all grow up and develop in exactly the same way. You know that."

Sister thought it over.

"But why is Tommy different?" she asked.

"Because, sweetie," said Mama, "God made all of us special. He made Tommy special in his own way. God has a plan for us all. He loves you and me and Tommy very much."

Sister thought she understood about God's love and about the specialness of everyone. But she still had questions.

"But …" she began.

Mrs. Bruin was listening.

"Maybe, Sister," she said, "God made Tommy different so he could teach us something."

"What do you mean?" asked Sister.

"Well, look at Tommy playing," said Mrs. Bruin. "What do you see?"

Tommy was running and laughing with Honey.

"He looks very happy," said Sister, smiling.

"Yes," said Mrs. Bruin. "There is a special joy in Tommy—a special kind of happiness. Maybe God wants us to see that joy and be joyful, too, just like Tommy."

Sister watched Tommy and Honey playing. They certainly were having a good time. Suddenly, Sister laughed and ran after them. Tommy and Honey screamed and shouted and ran away from her. Brother and Barry noticed and joined in.

The whole gang ran around and around, laughing and shouting.

Finally they all fell down on the grass together in a big heap. They were all very happy.

Papa called, "Food's on!" The cubs came running.

The Bruins and the Bear family sat down at the picnic table. Mr. Bruin said grace:

"Lord, thank you for the food we are about to eat, and thank you for sending our wonderful friend, Tommy, who gives us such joy, to visit this week. In your words:

'Whoever welcomes this little child in my name welcomes me; and whoever welcomes me welcomes the one who sent me.'

Amen."

"Amen," they all said and dug into that delicious food.

"Yum!" said Tommy, happily.

"Yum!" they all agreed.

# Activities and Questions from Brother and Sister Bear

Talk about it:

1.  Why were the Bruins going to the Bear family's house for the afternoon? What did the cubs do when they got there?
2.  Why was Sister curious about Lizzy's cousin, Tommy?
3.  Name three ways God made you special and three ways one of your closest friends is special.

Get out and do it:

1.  There are many things that make a person special ... it could be the color of their hair or a talent or skill they have. Take some time to recognize how special someone in your family is. For example, tell your mom she is the best cookie-baker ever or tell your sister her dancing makes you happy. Remember that these gifts all come from God.
2.  As a family, discuss what Mama meant when she said, "We are all a little different from each other. We don't all grow up and develop in exactly the same way." Talk about the differences you all see in each other and the kinds of things that make others special too. Then say a prayer together, thanking God for the gifts he has given each of you.